OPEN THROAT

OPEN THROAT

HENRY HOKE

MCD FARRAR, STRAUS AND GIROUX

NEW YORK

MCD
Farrar, Straus and Giroux
120 Broadway, New York 10271

Printed in the United States of America
First edition, 2023

Library of Congress Cataloging-in-Publication Data
Names: Hoke, Henry, 1983– author.
Title: Open throat / Henry Hoke.
Description: First edition. | New York : MCD / Farrar, Straus
    and Giroux, 2023.
Identifiers: LCCN 2023000110 | ISBN 9780374609870
    (hardcover)
Subjects: LCGFT: Novels.
Classification: LCC PS3608.O48275 O64 2023 |
    DDC 813/.6—dc23/eng/20230112
LC record available at https://lccn.loc.gov/2023000110

Our books may be purchased in bulk for promotional,
educational, or business use. Please contact your local
bookseller or the Macmillan Corporate and Premium
Sales Department at 1-800-221-7945, extension 5442, or
by email at MacmillanSpecialMarkets@macmillan.com.

www.mcdbooks.com • www.fsgbooks.com
Follow us on Twitter, Facebook, and Instagram at @mcdbooks

10   9   8   7   6   5   4   3   2   1

There is no creature whose inward being is so strong that it is not greatly determined by what lies outside it.

—GEORGE ELIOT, *Middlemarch*

OPEN THROAT

I've never eaten a person but today I might

I wake up in my thicket to the sound of whipcracks
and look out and see a bulky man in a brown leather
jacket and brown hat swinging the whip toward two
other people a man and a woman

the woman holds a phone up and says *you look just
like him oh my god*

the man with the whip smiles and cracks it again
and I feel something in the bottom of my stomach
that's not hunger

I also feel hunger

the man without the whip lies down on his back and
spreads his legs and lifts his feet up to the sky and
shouts *okay do it just flick 'em just lightly flick my
nuts*

the man with the whip snaps his arm back and
forward and the whip hits the dirt in front of the
lying down man and the lying down man says
yes yes

the woman presses her phone and says *be careful
those are my boys*

I try to understand people but they make it hard

the man on the ground is skinny and the woman
with the phone is skinny but the man holding the
whip is thick and his neck bulges against the collar
of his tan shirt and I can see a vein and hear the
blood running down through his arm and his arm
flexes and gets meaty every time he raises the whip

the whip hits the ground and kicks up dust and it
sounds like the torment of all big cats

fuck this guy

I can smell his insides

my mouth waters and the drool slides down and
soaks my paws

I smack my lips louder than the whip's crack and the
people stop like they heard me and the lying down
man stands up and the woman turns her phone in
my direction and the man with the whip holds the
whip at the ready

yeah I heard that says the woman like someone
asked her a question

I'm not scared of their eyes

I'm the same color as my thicket and the same color
as the ground

no one sees me unless I want them to

the whip makes the bulky man brave and he steps
slow toward me and squints and leans in with his
throbbing neck vein in full focus

my mouth opens and I judge the distance
between the man and his skinny friends and try to
decide if I can drag him into the thicket quick
enough

I wonder if they'll chase us or if they'll run away

it's been weeks since I've eaten anything bigger than a raccoon

I think of how many meals I can get out of this man and how if I store him down in the caves the vultures won't find him and I'll be able to come back over and over to eat a little more

I think of all the nights we'll spend together

this man and his guts and me

let's get food says the man as he coils the whip around his fist and pulls his neck away from the path of my teeth

the woman claps her hands and says *yeah I thought I was totally over brunch but I guess I'm not*

I watch them walk fast down the trail and I go to sleep because sleep takes my hunger away

when I wake up I hear the last of the day's
hikers passing my thicket

two girls with huge water bottles that bounce the
sunlight through the branches and into my eyes

it's not easy to sleep on an empty stomach but I
guess I did okay

one girl says *god I can't believe it's dark already*

I know we have to start starting earlier says the other

she takes a sip from her bottle and says *no matter
how much I say no and cancel stuff there's still no
time* and the first girl says *that's just your scare city
mentality you have to work on that*

*yeah I just you know this you know I don't like
change* says the second girl and the first girl says *of
course but we all live in scare city under capitalism so*

we all have to make an effort to deprogram a scare
city mentality as like our central driving force

their voices get lower and then I can't hear them
anymore and I yawn and stretch my paws out and
their water bottles vanish with their bodies in the
sunset

I shouldn't be here and neither should they

now that the hikers are gone I leave my thicket and
go down into the dry ravine where lots of water used
to flow and I eat bugs and suck at the little trickles to
make my thirst less

I remember the last rain and I remember I wasn't
happy about it but I don't know how long it's been
since

now I need water to come from the sky or anywhere
else

I need more than a dirty sip

I think of the girl hikers and the shiny bottles they
gulp out of and I paw the dirt for more caterpillars

and eat them and I know I have to find somewhere
new to drink

things are changing

a while ago I wouldn't fantasize about eating a
person

what the girls said makes sense

I'm not sure what a scare city mentality is

but I have it

here is called different things by different
people

mostly they say ellay but they also say the park or
hollywood

I hear that word a lot

I know I live below the hollywood sign because the
hikers say *oh look we're below the hollywood sign* and
they say *can we get all the way up there* and they ask
which letter would you jump off

I've been up there but at night lights come on and
it's too exposed so I stay down where I am now

views don't matter to me anyway

the hikers say things like *look at that view* or say
things like *we have to do this more often get up here
and get perspective*

what they see makes them point or stop and turn
and put their hands on their hips and breathe deep
but the distance they love is an out of focus blur
when I try to look where they're looking

all I can see is what's right in front of me

when the sun drops below the ridge I leave the dried up ravine and go to town

town is where my people live

there are four of them and they have three tents set up just a few layers back in the trees where the hikers can't see

but I see in the dark

the people in town smell familiar to me a smell like warmth or the woods not the sweet hiker smell that makes my head hurt

and that's how I found them a while ago and found their pile of trash and the smaller animals that come to eat their trash and offer themselves up to get eaten by me

the people build a fire some nights and I have to stay far away from the glow but they haven't done that in months they're afraid of the dryness like I'm afraid of the dryness

there's a water pump in the clearing past town and that's why they built town where they built it

it's not a bad setup

I go to the water pump and there's a deep puddle below it and I lap and lap and lap

I'm the secret member of town

I stay on the edges and don't mess with their tents or their tarps and supplies but I hear them talk about me

the older man in the left tent calls me puma

the couple in the middle tent call me ley own

the young man in the right tent calls me a different name every day but it always ends with cat

fucker cat or shitfuck cat or goddamn fuck cat

I can take it

he's kind otherwise and leaves his trash by a tree
and tonight it's a bucket of chicken bones but at
the bottom there's chicken

the meat and the bones taste like many people's
saliva and my stomach gets full and I get grateful
and my eyes fill

I want to thank my people but I know if they see me
it'll fuck up our relationship

the first light means it's time to go and I bring
a bone back to my thicket

the hikers start early and I hear voices as soon as I'm
settled in hidden and gnawing

or I hear one voice a man's voice

I'm a good listener says the man and I see he's with a
woman who hikes beside him

the man says *really I'm serious I want to listen
you can tell me anything you want about us or me
or the dinner anything I promise I'll just listen and
I won't interrupt or project I'll just I can take it you
don't know what a good listener I am without you
or when I'm not around you when I'm with other
people it's just this specific stuff with us that makes it
hard so I'm ready to listen I really am I promise I'm
ready*

this is my bedtime story today and I close my eyes
and leave my ears open

I'm a good listener

I don't hear the woman's voice and I start to wonder
what she sounds like

I wonder what I sound like

at dusk I feel alone enough

I chance a growl but the earth growls louder

the ground feels wrong my paws aren't attached
anymore

they give out

my body on the ground shudders and everything
shudders around me it's all moving at the same time
the mountain moves I feel like I'm in water there's
no foothold little rocks roll by the branches of my
thicket scratch my face in a way they're not
supposed to and the small sharp pain doesn't wake
me because I'm not asleep

I can't get up and I think I never will and this goes
on forever as the shudder ends

the stillness now is not the stillness before

I don't trust this stillness

there are small bits of blood on my legs from the branch scratches

my thicket isn't safe anymore

I step out and there's a person standing next to me

she's wearing a yellow shirt and yellow shoes and her back is turned and she's messing with her phone so she doesn't see me

I freeze and feel awful

okay okay she shouts into the air and then says again to herself *okay*

she steps back on one foot and her shoe is so close to my face I can smell it

the phone is up at her ear now and she scratches her side and leaves her hand there holding on to herself tight while she talks

did you feel that she says into the phone

no she says *no I'm in the park I don't know I walk
now what*

her shoe moves away from my face and then she gets
quiet and listens and then she shouts *how did you
not feel it it's a fucking earthquake*

and then she gets quieter and says *babe I know you
said not to call but I'm calling because look fuck it
I'm coming home*

she snorts and wipes something away from her eyes
with the back of her phone hand

she runs forward down the hill and dust from her
yellow shoes hangs in the air along with the word
earthquake

I look down and touch one front paw to the other to
make sure I'm real and alive

I've felt so many shudders before but either this one
was different or I'm different

now

I scrape the dirt and walk uphill but I'm worried the
ground won't ever be solid again

it's dark when I reach the caves and I get lucky
because the earthquake has pushed a swarm of bats
out of one tunnel and they swoop and scatter above
me and they're just as confused as I am

even the shudder can't destroy my nightly
hunger

I use their confusion

they have no idea how high I can jump

I leap and swat one bat down from the air and crack
its neck with my teeth and then I do the same with
another and another

this easy hunt is like a game and I find joy in the
new moonlight

I go deep into the caves until they get so narrow I
have to stop

if more shudders are coming I want to be
somewhere small

I turn and lie down with my bat snack in front of me
and fill my mouth and then my stomach and there's
water dripping so I wash down the wings

I've heard hikers talk about earthquakes before they
say *it's a reason to get the fuck out of ellay* or they say
they're not bad anymore or *it's not a thing anymore
the fault totally shifted*

anyway it's better to be outside when the big one hits
they say

I'm always outside

tonight under layers of rock I'm full and I can at
least breathe

but even here in the cave I know I'm still outside I'm
not in a tent like the people in town and it doesn't
make it better that the shudder happened and
won't make it better if it happens again

I don't know

it's hard to say how it feels

I'm looking for the words

piss splashes my face and wakes me up

the sharp smell bristles my fur and my eyes pop
open

I watch the man's dangling part and the wet pouring
from it onto the pebbles in front of me

the salt covers my lips and I lick it away

I'm hungry again

I turn away from the spray and my eyes must catch
the sunlight because the pissing man makes a deep
noise and clutches his chest and turns before pulling
up his pants and he skids on the gravel and falls on
his face

he recovers and runs out of the cave and doesn't
look back

if he looked back he'd see me not chasing

not moving

he'd see me not giving a fuck

I've been pissed on before

I stand and leave my cranny and sniff his puddle
and straddle it and piss and the puddle gets larger

I can still smell his fear

I walk over to where he fell and paw the frantic
marks he made in the gravel and I think

what it would be like to hunt him

he was so close when he woke me up and I had all
the power of surprise on my side

the attack could've happened right then and I could
stuff him in the cranny and I'd be set for a few meals

he had a scrawny neck that'd snap in a sec

but he had no meat to him

nothing like the man with the whip

I'm only thinking all this because the pissing man
is gone

and I know I won't see him again

I find his phone by the mouth of the cave

it's black and shiny and has a pattern like snakeskin
and I flip it over and press on it like I see the people
pressing on theirs but

phones don't work for me

I can't pick it up and raise it right up to my face or
my ear and anyway

who would I call what would I say where would my
voice go

I lean close and see something in the black
screen

maybe a tongue and teeth

my reflection

but I don't have that word yet

my eyes

I like to think the man who ran will remember
these eyes

always

I swat the phone over by the metal base of a sign

the sign stands at the entrance to the cave and when
I see people here the people stop and move close and
look at it and then they either turn around or go
inside

I don't know what this sign is because I can't read

there are signs all over the park and I watch people
stop at them and I try to figure out what the signs
say by the people's reactions

sometimes people ask each other what they say like
they can't read either but it's because one is always
closer to the sign and then they help me by reading
out loud

so I know the one that says fire danger very
high today and the one that says caution
rattlesnakes

I don't have a problem with rattlesnakes

the one that says fire danger changes color and
sometimes the people read it and say *extreme* and
then say *shit*

is there a warning sign for me

is it this one

when I leave the cave the birds are screaming and
there's an ever bigger sound in the sky

whirring and grinding and moving in long
circles

the young man in town calls them fucking
helicopters

the fucking helicopters circle at night and shine big
lights down that take away my dark and then I can't
see and I can't stay hidden

the young man in town will leave his tent and
scream and shake his fist and call them names
like he calls me

he hates them so I hate them

the whirring and grinding sound gets lower and I
hear hikers coming and run behind a tree

the hikers are looking up of course and one says
that's a rescue chopper

yeah for the children's hospital says the other *they're
always going to the children's hospital down on sunset
I hear them all day*

oh perfect the first hiker says *now whenever I look up
and see them or hear them I'll just think of the bloody
and dying baby in there and that'll make me feel
great*

I look up through the branches of the big tree but
the sky is too bright for me to see anything except
painful light

instead I shut my eyes and listen to the fucking
helicopter sound fade

I imagine the bloody sky children

I think about blood raining from the sky and I roll
onto my back and stretch and claw the air and open
my mouth and think of catching all the blood rain
in my mouth and it quenching my thirst and
making it go away in a way it hasn't since I was
small

when I'm hungry I think about blood too much

also when I'm not hungry

I lick the little scratches my thicket made on me and
taste dirt and my own insides and it's not quenching
at all it tastes like cat and I'm cat and I don't like cat

I stand up and spit and shake my head and grow up

I probably wouldn't eat a child

my new thicket is a nest of twisted trees above
a path

hikers come by all day while I rest but I'm ten feet
above them and they never suspect

from here I wouldn't even have to leap I'd just have
to drop and whichever hiker I wanted would be
mine

I try to keep these thoughts from my head and let
the dry breeze cause sleep

the hikers talk about their therapists

they decide what is good or bad about their
therapists and decide if the therapist helped them
feel good or bad and they throw these two words
around like they have different meanings

a therapist is something I want

I don't know if I feel good or bad

if feeling hungry is bad then I almost always feel
hungry so maybe I almost always feel bad

a therapist can help me with this

a therapist can explain why I have a shudder inside
after the shudder outside is over

a hiker says *I pay her two hundred a session just to
talk shit about my parents*

my mother gave me a name I can't share

I'm not from ellay I just ended up here

I was a baby far away where the sun sets

a deep forest on the edge of the water where we
could taste the salt carried up by the wind at night

we

because there were many of us in the green hill
where the colors were colors I don't see here and the

deer roamed for us to capture and all we had to do
was lie in wait and be patient

my mother could stay still for days and listen for the
soft sounds prey makes

my mother was very kind

her bloodthirst was insatiable

she taught me how to snap a neck with my jaws

why would I ever leave her

my father gave me a name I won't repeat

he wasn't around in our part of the forest he kept his
own territory higher up in the hillside

when we traveled toward the water we would
sometimes see him lurking and watching us to make
sure we remembered to worship him even if we were
doing all the traveling and killing ourselves

my mother stood on the uphill side and blocked my
little body from his view

I grew from kitten size to my now size and
stayed close to my mother while all the other
cats went away to find their own thickets
and stalk their own prey and make their own
kittens

my father wanted more and so his territory grew
and we were suddenly in it

he came down the hill

I was too big then for my mother to block

he attacked her first

a father to a kitten is an absence

a grown cat to a father is a threat

a hiker says *my only really good therapist was in
new york*

of course says the other hiker

they talk about new york a lot in ellay

in new york you don't need a car

cars are loud metals that carry people to the park
and that they leave in lines and clusters near the
paths and that they can't stop talking about needing
but not in new york

is new york where I have to go

from what people say it sounds like everyone there is
coming here and that's why everything is changing
or why everything costs too much now or why all
the good things about ellay are disappearing

I want to do the opposite I want to go to a place
where I won't be hated

where there are therapists running around
everywhere like deer and I can just find one and
catch it and pin it down

store it somewhere safe and visit it once a week

that's the thing with ellay says the other hiker *forget
about therapy you have to go to the next level here*

all we've got here is gurus

their smell leaves my nose

my mother taught me to hunt but my father taught
me to be hunted

after the attack he chased me toward the sunrise

staying uphill from me all the time so I wouldn't
forget his power

when I had to shit I'd do my best to bury it and not
leave a trace

the only direction I could go where I knew my father
wouldn't follow was toward the roar of the long death

every animal was afraid of the long death

even my father

at the top of the farthest hill I saw more hills
hills with no green

but between where I was and the place I had to go
was the long death

the long death was a giant blurry path that led all
the way up and all the way down and was always
blazing with fast moving cars that killed countless
creatures

I traded old fear for new fear

I have trouble sleeping in the twisted trees
because there are so many hikers who go by
and talk loud all day

they talk about how no one in ellay has real jobs but
from what they describe as real jobs I don't think
they have them either

ellay is a mecca for the underemployed they say

to be employed they need skills

they say to each other *you've got so many marketable
skills*

I go over my skills

my skills are hiding so long that you forget I'm there

watching and listening until I memorize your habits
and your language but

killing is my job

a big lizard crawls by and I

smash its head against a rock and swallow half of it

that's trauma too that's the trauma talking says a girl
on a phone *it's all trauma*

she goes silent and she stuffs her phone into a bag
hanging from her shoulder and when she pulls her
arm out a piece of green paper flutters to the ground
behind her

I know the paper is important because I've seen
people drop it before and they say *shit* and they run
and grab it and they say *that was close*

the trauma girl doesn't do any of that she doesn't
even notice that it fell and she keeps going and I wait
and the moon appears above me

I jump down and pick up the paper in my teeth

I try to taste its importance

nothing

I decide my people will get more use out of the green
paper so I take it to town

they may have made it through the earthquake
and they may have tents to keep out the cold and the
rain and they may have piles of trash but I want to
contribute

this may be their town but we all live in scare city

there's a dog in town tonight and I stop before I get
too close

dogs don't do it for me

when their people bring them up the mountain they
always sniff out my hiding spots and bark

and I can't eat them because the one dog I ate once
was dead already and it made my insides feel awful
for days

so just the thought and the sound are sickening

this dog is tied up outside the middle tent and barking

but not at me

I'm too far away

too good at my special skills

I let the green paper fall out of my mouth

the dog is facing the other direction

in the trees beyond the dog I see three sets of eyes

coyotes are different

they run together and have a mentality like mine

if I don't eat them they get ideas they start to think
they can eat me if there are enough of them and
enough bites to take

these three have their lit up eyes fixed on the dog
and they're ready for blood

so I get around behind them and tackle one and
crunch its neck and the other two run away

I drag the skinny body to the water pump and drink
from the puddle and eat from the coyote

the dog stops barking

you're welcome I think to my sleeping people

people are attached to their dogs

in my triumph I sleep and in my sleep I dream
and in my dream I see the man with the whip and
his bulging neck vein

the vein grows larger than me and larger than the
mountain

I'm so full at sunrise that I forget to leave

a voice says *dead dog* and then the voice repeats it
dead dog

the young man has a bottle in his hand and he's
standing on the other side of the eaten coyote

there's a bucket lying on the ground

the young man says it again *dead dog* and his neck
twitches and his voice changes and he says *lots of
low level parking*

like he knows what scares me most is what I don't
understand

he raises the bottle

would we be okay if I had the green paper in my
mouth instead of coyote guts

if I had something to offer

bad cat

he throws the bottle and it hits my front paw hard
and I tip sideways and he runs uphill and all the
ground dirt floats in the air of the bad morning and
I watch it blow away and the young man stops and
turns and looks down at me to make sure I'm going

he looks at me like my father

I return to the twisted trees and the path
below is busy again

I'm kind of a poet says some boy kid to another boy
kid he's holding hands with

when they ask what are you says the kid *my mind
goes right to poet cuz I don't ever make the obvious
choice I make the deep choice I want to claim that
title poet poet ha ha*

I watch their hands while they walk away

hands that could be grabbing bottles and throwing
but instead are wrapped together and connected

I think I'm kind of a poet

because when I finally find a deer left behind by a
herd

its leg broken and stuck in a rock

even though I know I shouldn't

know it'll make the meat spoil quicker

I eat the heart first

I drag my deer to the twisted trees where it'll be covered so I can make the meat and iron flavor that's filling my mouth last

this is a feast for a week

I won't need my people and their tents and their scraps

won't need to go to town

I can take care of myself

it's easy to lie when I'm stuffed

rest tries to find me

but the nonstop voices of the passing hikers find me instead

yeah I can't wait to see you a man says into wires
that hang from his ears

so let's not wait right with every step we take with
what you do when you hang up and when you dream
you're moving closer to me and I'm doing the same
we're not waiting not standing and waiting we're
constantly traveling in time toward when we get to
be together again

there's something wrong with my ears

I can't shut them like I can shut my eyes

more and more voices come and I stop looking to
see where they're all coming from

we don't have earthquake insurance they say

but we've always got a go bag packed in case fire
comes down the mountain

they don't know where they are

they keep changing the name

is it ellay

or is it beachwood

or is it the canyon

they call everything a disaster

I stare at the trees because the trees don't talk

this is not a big deal they all say but only before they say other things

this is not a big deal but the car's gonna need way more work than they thought

this is not a big deal but he ghosted me whatever he's ugly and all his friends suck

this is not a big deal but right now I need you to listen to me

they say *I can't believe it's almost the fourth and I still don't have a check from him I've been looking at the mailbox every single day* and they say *you know what the definition of insanity is doing the same thing over and over* and they say *yeah but checking the mail*

they say *ni modo* and then they say it again

they say *fame is a real killer all I did was one
commercial and now I get recognized and shouted at
god I need to go back to being nobody*

they say *yeah of course the project is gay everything is
gay now everything is gay now it's all gay everything
is gay now*

they say *no I'm not going to tell her*

I want to devour their sound

I have so much language in my brain

and nowhere to put it

I spend half the night dragging my deer up the hill
to the clifftop

to find some quiet

when I reach the top there's an owl perched on the
rock across from me

it's not interested in my deer

the meat's been unmoving for too long

the owl's head turns to look at me so I look back into
its eyes and I see what it sees

the bright world below the park at night is a blur to
me when I try to look out over it

but if I get close enough to a creature's eye I can see
what it sees and in the owl's eye I see ellay clearly

more lights than I could ever count stretch out into
the darkness and don't stop stretching

I'm scared of how far they go

I get why people can't decide on one name

this can't all be ellay

with a stomach full of deer I walk uphill

there are no eyes on me anymore

I feel watched

a whirring sound pops out of a bush and I look for a
bird but a flash of light hits me instead

I blink and go tear up the bush and inside is a black
box standing up on little black sticks and it whirs
and clicks and flashes again and this time it hurts
my eyes and takes my sight away

in the blindness a cold wind cuts into the skin below
my fur

when my sight comes back I go close to the black
box again and I see my nose and mouth in the little
glass circle and I think of the people holding up
their phones and pressing and pressing

I step back and wait for the next flash but there's no
next flash

my claws come out and I knock the little black sticks
and the black box tilts and falls and it pops open like
a trap

what did it capture

the smell of easy prey wakes me

what I see when I open my eyes isn't something to eat

it's two slow people withered and wrapped in layers
of clothing

one is hunched over and the other staggers and
helps him up the trail

it's sweet but unappetizing

I can smell their death coming at me through the
woods

is this what the coyotes smell when they circle

what my father smelled on me

what made him want to snap my neck in his jaws or
beat my head on the ground

was I a threat

or just on my way out

my skin is starting to get loose and some of my fur
drags and tugs on things it didn't drag or tug on
before

it's okay

old is fine

I'm old because I'm not dead

something explodes above me

the sun's already set but this brings the day back
white and blinding in the black sky like a swarm of
fucking helicopters

there are cheers rising from down below like all of
ellay is making this happen like the people forgot
how dry my life is

and they do it again and again

more explosions and cheers and less night

I look down to stop my eyes from hurting but the
light doesn't go anywhere and now the bursts are in
my ears too

I hear the sky crackle and fall down around me

all I feel is fire danger

this is too much

the shudder inside becomes unbearable

I can't eat everything I'm afraid of

the horror of the sky fire stays in my head for days

I sit secluded on my cliff where no one comes until sundown

two men approach the cave below and I watch

they walk a few feet apart and stare at their phones

and don't talk

the only sound they make is footsteps on gravel

at the mouth of the cave one stops and looks at the sign and one doesn't and keeps walking in

the space between them grows larger

when they're out of sight I climb down the cliff

and creep to the cave mouth where I can watch the
men and not be seen

their phones are gone now and one stands close
behind the other and leans in to the other's neck to
bite

the best deer I ever ate was one I didn't kill

when I made it far enough away that my father
stopped hunting

he left me to the long death with its roar that got
louder with every step I took

I first saw the deer bolting through the woods and it
stopped in front of me

stopped long enough for another big cat to catch it

I watched and did nothing as the other big cat ended
the deer's life and made it meat

with blood on his mouth and nose and whiskers the
other big cat looked at me

a challenge to approach

or an invitation

I waited until he'd eaten a bite of intestine and then
joined

my face buried in the deer and my eyes on him

when you meet a big cat who will share a kill you
can't let go of him easily

I bend low and enter the mouth of the cave and hide
in the shadows

the men are on the ground now

on their knees and the one in front has his hands
planted flat like my paws against the dirt

there's a hot scent where they're connecting

my eyes are full

the motion they make reminds me of the shudder
but in a way that makes it okay

they move like the whole cave wants them to move
like a natural part of this world

the man behind collapses forward and his front
joins with the other man's back and their arms wrap
together

the shape they form is like my shape

their breathing is hard but their bodies are
motionless and they go silent and my purr echoes

I'm loud

they're going to see me

I remember how every day the kill sharer and I
would meet by his deer and bloody our faces
together

and each bite that made the carcass smaller made
the roar of the long death smaller too

I would stay close and he would go off somewhere
and return matted and hungry his teeth bared as if
he had stories he wanted to tell me but couldn't and
his chewing was enough and I treasured the way he
blew air out of his nostrils

no deer lasts as long as you want it to

I saved him the final bite and I waited and waited
but he didn't return and then I knew it was time I
crossed the long death

the long death up close and in focus was even harder
to take with its lights and speeding murderous cars
never stopping on their hell ride to the right and to
the left

I spent all night terrified and slinking along the side
daring myself to cross and when the light broke over
the hill I saw the body of the kill sharer

his fur coated in a mix of dried deer blood and wet
cat blood his own blood

I ran straight across the long death my feet
determined and pounding because I wanted
to die

I'm not that lucky

the men in the cave pull their pants up and get back
on their phones

the one behind leaves first and the other one waits a
moment and follows

they're so into their screens that neither of them
sees me

I go over to the spot on the ground where the men
were connecting and lie down in the disturbed dirt

my body twists into the same position the kill sharer
had in death

I wonder if I'd been brave enough and tried to cross
first

would he have found my body

or if we'd crossed together would we both have
made it

I imagine the kill sharer appearing now at the
mouth of the cave

circling like I'm his prey and pouncing and
connecting with me and the warmth we would
make together with our eight paws and two
dangling parts and four rows of teeth

I get up and crouch and shit and bury what came
out of me

two more men approach and these two brought
their voices and their voices say *man I don't want
you to miss your chance* and say *yeah god she's so
cute*

they pass the mouth of the cave and they don't come
in and the cave is fully dark now and I feel hidden
and I watch

they kick rocks and pace and push small sticks in
their mouths and the sticks make a glow and the
men blow out smoke and the glowing sticks
shrink

I know these men

the man with the whip and his skinny friend

the man with the whip is not holding a whip and
he's not wearing a hat or jacket but I know his
thickness and I know that neck vein I've been seeing
in my head since he first leaned it within reach of
my teeth

*this is your chance to have pancakes with
allison* says the skinny friend to the man with the
whip

she wants pancakes what can I say says the man with
the whip

they are not going to connect

I follow them down the trail and they reach the trees
near town

just ask her when we get back says the skinny friend
hold on I have to take a piss

the skinny friend ducks into the woods and leaves
the man with the whip alone

I go closer and the man with the whip stretches his
arms above his head and spits on the ground and
the extended length of him looks vulnerable

but the skinny friend runs back out and says *shit
never mind* and the man with the whip says *what*
and the skinny friend says *there's a whole y'know
camp in there* and he points through the trees to
where the tents of town are

fuck says the man with the whip *these fuckin' tents
are everywhere now man I mean my street's not safe*

and the skinny friend says *yeah julia doesn't wanna*
walk over anymore they take up the whole sidewalk
and the man with the whip says *fuckin' disgusting*
with what we pay in rent

they go quiet and the man with the whip pulls a
small metal box out of his pocket and holds it up

alright fuck 'em he says *seriously watch this*

he flicks the metal box open and it makes fire

another weapon

he walks with the weapon into town

I crouch behind a tree and the skinny friend stands
back near me and says *what*

the man with the whip turns and says *shh* and he
goes to the pile of trash near the tents and he makes
the fire and holds it against the trash and the trash
becomes little bits of fire too

he squats and steps over to the cardboard outside
the young man's tent and makes the fire again

from his little metal box and the cardboard turns bright

the man with the whip closes the metal box and sprints to the skinny friend

smoke 'em out says the man with the whip and pats the skinny friend on the back and they walk away quick making nervous laughing sounds

ha ha ha ha

I watch the fire lick the tents and I hear my people wake up

the couple in the middle make muffled noises

a spark jumps to the brush at the bottom of a tree and the flames rise and light everything

this is a big deal

the woman of the couple tears out of their tent with her dog and the man follows and tosses her a backpack and she turns and looks at the flames and the man goes and pulls the old man in the left tent

out and the old man staggers backward and leans on
a tree right next to me coughing

the woman shouts *santo* and she picks up a bucket
and throws the bucket at him and he catches it and
runs up the hill toward the water pump

the dog goes barking past me out of sight and they
don't try to chase him

the woman waves a hand from her head to her heart
and from shoulder to shoulder

the cardboard by the right tent burns fast and the
fire consumes the young man's tent and when he
steps out his legs and arm are on fire

the old man and the woman don't move so I move

I go past them and toward the right tent and I leap
on the young man and knock him to the ground on
his back and I pound the fabric of his jacket where
the fire is and knock it out and I grab his collar with
my teeth and pull him away from the cardboard and
the cardboard is almost gone and the tent is all
flames and I pound with my paws again on his legs

this time and one fire goes out and the other doesn't
and his mouth is open he is probably screaming but
I only hear the crackle of burning trees and it is
hotter than I can take

I don't want my story to end here

I roll the young man on his face and then back onto
his back trying to cover his fire leg in dirt

something hits me

the old man throws another rock and this one hits
the young man but I see he's aiming for my face

the woman screams *aguas* and she grabs a large
branch from the ground and steps forward and
jabs at me and another rock from the old man clips
my ear

the man returns clutching his bucket and when he
sees me he drops it and water sloshes out and tears
fill his eyes the bucket is so small and the flames are
almost done destroying our town

the stick and more rocks come at me through the
smoke and I feel one bounce hard off my spine

the young man's fire is out now but he's crying in
pain

I step off him and turn and run away from my
people

away from their doom and toward the lights of a
larger one

the flames rise to the tops of the trees behind me
and the hills in front of me reflect the glow and they
might as well be burning too

fire is the only future

the burn is behind me but the smoke is everywhere

without the sun or moon I don't know when day stops or night starts

I can't tell how long I've been walking away

walking not running because I can't see what's right in front of me anymore and can't see myself

I could be something else I could be a deer or even a person

but not a bird a bird could rise above the smoke

I can't sing

my lungs are full of ugly

I look down and there are no paws

any sec I could step off a cliff

I think I've always felt this way

the smoke makes it clear

today tomorrow or yesterday

I'm fully empty

my hunger joins up with my cough and I go from
walking to crawling

voices come at me through the smoke

oh he's gotten much worse says a voice *since the
election he's in front of the teevee twenty four seven
and it's just see en en from morning till night and you
know he pretends it upsets him but I think he loves it
loves all the jokes and the hate and the chaos I mean I
think he secretly or you know repressedly loves the
guy you know and loves all the nonstop media
coverage*

yeah says another voice *he wants to fuck the
president*

I know these voices are a memory and not a now

moving doesn't seem worth it and I stop and lie
down with my not body and wait for something
anything to shift

the memory voices leave me and the smoke stays
and I close my eyes

I picture the men in the cave but they're on fire and
I'm running from them

today tomorrow or yesterday

the wind changes direction and I get my body back

I put one paw in front of the other

in the burnt but open air I'm the only creature still
living

I reach a clearing and there's a checkered blanket
laid out and an overturned basket

things left by fleeing people

the basket is empty

I dig in a knocked over can nearby but there's only
plastic and more plastic

it's on the ground too

I'm not sure how to have a body again after losing it
and my desire goes in all directions

slow and starved and wanting to connect

fuck

down the hill from the clearing is a street and near
the street is a giant round tent with no sides

underneath I see animals

I get closer and the animals are frozen

not from fear

of me

but because they're fake

they're painted and hard and arranged in a circle

a deer and a white horse with a horn and a big cat
with a fiery swirl of hair around its yawning mouth

they're all impaled and I go and stand with them
and expect my own impalement

the rod dropping from above and stabbing through
me and holding me in place

giving me purpose

it's the middle of the day and I'm in the middle of a
field and I don't feel exposed

what person would walk into a scorched
world

I follow the street and enjoy the dead silence of a
park abandoned by everything that flies and
shouts

until a sound stops me

faint but frightening

an unending roar I could never forget

another long death

I crouch by a tree and wait for the sun to set at my
back to make sure I'm facing the right way and yes
I'm facing the right way and that means the park has
an end and there's no more escape

I can't do another crossing

I'm not about to die on an empty stomach

what good would that do

tonight I can smell so many animals it makes
me angry

all it took was a short walk downhill to catch their
scent

I'm never going toward the sunrise again

or the sunset

and the mountains are uphill so my nose takes me
in the only remaining direction

and it leads me to the stench and a wall of metal
poles reaching higher up than my head can look

I expect the animals I smell to be impaled here too

alive this time not fake alive and dripping blood that
I can lick and lick from the metal

instead the poles are clean and I can't fit between
them

I go to the top of a ridge where the poles stop and
leap down onto a hard path between strange trees a
kind of tree that doesn't grow on the other side of
the wall

the howling starts

now these animals can smell me back

I see a deep pool of blue water and run toward it and
let my tongue out to lap

but my tongue and face stop short at a hard wall

a wall I can see through but can't move through

all I taste is the smeared fingerprints of people

there are writhing hairy animals swimming in the
water on the other side

anxious bodies that don't know I can't reach them

I turn and follow the path and hit another clear wall

behind this one is a god shadow perched on a
cracked limb

its wings spread bigger than three vultures
combined

the god shadow flaps and I pray for it to fly and find
a dead thing and circle and show me where it's
rotting I'm so starved I'd eat the most rotting thing
the most dead thing

the bird looks up and in its eyes I see netting
stretched tight across the night sky

it's going nowhere

what is this place

every ten steps I take I'm at a new net or a new
clear wall and there's a new animal somewhere
behind it and some shriek or some rustle erupts as
I pass

my senses can't keep up

I leap up onto a low stone wall and smell something
like me but unlike me

I look down into this new area and it doesn't have a
net or clear wall it just goes deep

there are cat eyes by a small stream below and the
eyes meet my eyes and judge my power

this big cat has stripes running up and down its
body like claw marks like it's been shredded

there's water dripping from its mouth and it dares
me to jump down and drink

I know this look it's the look a coyote gives me when
it knows there are other coyotes hiding in the brush
or circling behind me

I leave the big cat's evil sight

have fun in your trap

I'll show you a predator

beyond a murky green pond that even I won't drink
from my nostrils catch an irresistible scent

small and sick and afraid

three of my favorite flavors

I leap another wall and this area isn't so deep so I
fall toward the smell

a fat furry gray thing clutches a tree and extends its
weird little tongue and before its squeal hits my ears
my teeth hit its neck and I pull it to the ground and
end its life and my starvation

every bite tastes bad

the body slowly becomes bones and now I'm alone

a spotlight hits the ground next to me and the blood
on my paws shines and I gag

there are people on the way

they won't understand

people don't have to kill things like I have to kill
things

I jump as high as my stuffed body will allow and I
scramble to the top of the wall

a voice shouts *oh jesus kiki*

a woman in a hat enters a gate below and waves a
man over

they stand over the bones I left and the woman says
to the bones *poor kiki*

I'm sorry kiki

they shouldn't have named you

the man points at me and I remember I'm visible

running makes my head hurt but I run

there are people shouts on all sides of me

more names

I run for the lights of ellay

even when I leave the park the park comes
with me

the burn smell stays on my fur and in my nose and
the trees continue and get split by the curving street
and stand tall on either side and I choose the side
with the most green and hug the hedges and try to
go fast

there are buildings here much bigger and stronger
than the tents in town and their doors are hard not
soft

they go up and up almost as tall as the trees

I hear a car approaching and I disappear into a thick
hedge

two men step out of the car and they make noise
with long sticks that end in spinning blades like tiny
fucking helicopters and they stand across the street

and drag the blades across the hedges sending pieces
of green flying up in the air

it's so green here

how

I bury myself deeper in case the men get tired of
their hedge and attack mine

but they don't

when the spinning goes away I look out and see two
small hikers

a man and a woman I know from the park

they step over the huge roots that pop out of the
ground on their way up the hill

don't they get that the park isn't safe now

they stop in front of me like they heard my thoughts
like they heard my warning

you know who lives there says the woman and she
points across the street to the building beyond the
trimmed hedge *that's slaughter's house*

the man takes a big swig from his water bottle and
says *oh fuck really I love slaughter or y'know I loved
him he's like a legend*

yeah says the woman *but his wife is younger than you*

gross says the man

gross yeah says the woman *but fully typical*

they continue to walk uphill toward danger and
there's nothing I can do to stop them

I look at the house where they pointed

the name slaughter sounds good to me

like something I could do

like somewhere I belong

I nap until night and wake to a car coming to life
and pulling out from in front of the slaughter house

the car lights blind me for a sec and when I can see
again I cross the street and crawl through the
trimmed hedge and into the thick green grass

water sprays up out of small holes in the ground and
I drink until I hear another car

I run around the side of the house into an even
larger grassy area in the back

when I get there I see a girl in a cloak on her knees
lit by a blue lantern in a circle of sparkling stones
and she holds a bowl and the bowl pushes smoke
into the air

she lays the bowl on the ground in front of her and
puts her head down so the cloak covers everything
except her long hair and her long hair spills and
licks the grass like a flame

it's a color I didn't think I could see until now

she keeps her head down and I sneak by and hug the
edge of the house

I can hear her whispering

around another corner I find a hole in the hard gray
stone where there's one chunk missing and it's just
big enough for my body so I squeeze my body inside

I have to keep my head low but I smell mice and I
crawl in the dirt toward their scent and the sound of
scuttles

a mouse and a bunch of baby mice run toward my
mouth and my mouth eats them

with my stomach full I keep moving and the farther
under the slaughter house I go the lower the dirt
sinks and the larger the space above me becomes

there's another me sized hole in another layer of
gray stone and on the other side of this hole I can
stand up all the way

the ground slants down into a ditch and at the edge
of the ditch is a wall and at the top of the wall is a
wooden platform with a wooden railing and a door
and beyond the door is light

I take it all in

this is my first room

there's a dripping pipe on one side of the ditch and it
gives me all the water I could want

I sleep for what feels like days here in this dark safe
spot where the sun doesn't rise or set

confused mice come back from the outside world
and run through the low space and down into my
ditch and before they even see me I trap them in my
jaws

nothing's ever been so easy

I forget the scent of the burning forest

my fur smells like earth again

my ears hear the dripping and the clicking of bugs
and then they hear shouts

a man's deep voice coming from somewhere above

this must be slaughter

I go back through the hole into the low space where
my head touches the surface above me and my ears
are close to the inside of the house and the voice
becomes clear

muffled by a floor is the right volume for people

everything went fine says slaughter *they're just gonna
keep her there for a few days until they know
everything's still working okay with her body*

for a moment I listen to slaughter listen

yeah I mean sure he's fine he's alive he's a baby

I follow slaughter's footsteps to the edge of the low
space

slaughter pounds on a wall and says a short name

I hear another voice and something in this other
voice sounds kind of like slaughter but higher and
younger

like a little slaughter

the voice says *dad* and the way it says dad is the way
most people say no

I curl up and let the bouncing shouts become my
lullaby

these are my new people

they don't know it

there's sunlight coming from the hole in the
bottom of the house

so I can tell it's day

slaughter continues his shouting

people are loud during the day and quiet at
night

I roll on my back and listen to slaughter as he steps
in a circle on the floor above me and I know without
seeing that he's on a phone because he sounds like
everyone in the park when they hold their phones to
their heads or speak into their wires

*no we're fine now the house is out of the danger area
and anyway it's all out* says slaughter *but did you see
they figured out the whole fire started in a homeless
camp*

slaughter goes quiet and I hear the sound of a bottle hitting metal and then he says *this is what happens when we let them just live up there and no one does anything about it*

his voice keeps me awake

but slaughter is a comfort

if the mice run out I can always eat him

the light leaves the hole and a possum appears and does what possums do

I grab it and make it mine and drag it back to my ditch and dig my teeth into its middle

it tastes okay but I'm distracted from my meal by the hard footsteps and slamming above and I go back into the low space

slaughter says *alright I'm leaving for the hospital last chance* and then he asks *you're not coming*

slaughter says *fine you're not coming*

slaughter says *don't come*

a door slams and then another door slams

a woman's voice pours through the floor

not a real woman no a woman in a recording
singing beside music and thumps

she sings *living alone is all I've ever done well*

I go back to my possum but before I can bite a bigger
thing happens

the door above me opens

a square of light hits my ditch

a person steps onto the wooden platform with a
small stick held to her mouth

little slaughter blows smoke and the smoke fills the
air above me and blocks her face

all I see is the flame hair from the backyard

she's not wearing a cloak anymore just a big shirt

when the cloud clears she's looking right at me

in my whole life I've been seen by only a few people
and each time was a failing of my stealth and my
mother's lessons

but this moment is not like those moments

my gaze meets hers and I don't feel guilty for being
seen

there's not even a whiff of fear

I summoned you says little slaughter

and in our eyes it feels right

stay says little slaughter and I do

she goes back out the door and a moment later the
music stops and I realize I'm waiting for her to
return

she returns and she has a handful of shredded goo
and she tosses the goo down to me

I leave my possum and go to the goo and sniff it and
it's meat and I lick it and it's tasty

there you go heckit says little slaughter and then she
says *eww*

she wipes her hand on her shirt

I'm vegan says little slaughter *or I'm trying to be*

as I eat I keep my eyes on her

I want her to know I'm grateful

good girl heckit says little slaughter *I'm so glad you're
here*

she kneels and watches me chew and this unhunted
food is too easy

I love it

time goes by and I hear slaughter come in and shout and then go out again

and when he goes out again little slaughter comes to visit me

good morning heckit she says and she throws me meat

her daily offering

she holds out a large water bottle and pours and I go to the trickle and catch the liquid in my mouth and little slaughter smiles and doesn't stop pouring until the bottle is empty and as the container quenches my thirst I get why the hikers carry them

I try to make sense of the word she keeps saying *heckit* and after a few days of feedings I realize she's giving me a name *heckit*

I'll take it

I can't tell her my real one

my mother gave it to me when she first saw me lick
blood off my lips

it's not made of noises a person can make

now that my water supply is endless the sky
decides to rain

I watch it pour down through the crack in the low
space and the dirt beneath me becomes mud and
little creeks form

my lack of thirst makes me hate the water and I
leave the low space and when I get to my ditch I
watch the creeks wash down into it

my paws get wet and then the legs above the paws
get wet and then my dangling part and the
underside of my belly get wet

each time I shake myself dry more water rushes in

I claw the edges of the ditch but I can barely get a
grip and each new motion feels useless

where was this water when we needed it

when it could have helped

my paws catch a dry spot and I lift myself out of the
ditch

the weight of the water on my fur wears me out and
I find the driest corner and curl up and let the
rhythm of drops put me to sleep

I wake up because I'm drowning

the water's above my head and there are no dry
spots left on the ground

I kick against the wall and roll onto my back and
float and push water out of my nose and grab a
hard breath but I'm too soaked to stay on the surface
and my soak pulls me down to the bottom of the
room

in the dark water I see the hole to the low space and
it's also underwater

there's no way outside

I think of the creatures I saw swimming and try to
make their movements with my front legs

the water splashes but I don't rise

with every flail I think of every bad move I've made
to get to this moment

I see my mother lying still beneath my father and I
see the kill sharer lying still beside the long death
and I see my own body lying still in the flood

with my last breath I think the word please

let me start over

a hard object hits my back and I claw my way
onto it

a wood plank rising up like a ramp to the platform
and the railing above

I walk three steps and leap to the platform and
knock little slaughter backward and she lets go of
the plank

I crouch and cough out water and little slaughter
says *shh* and she grips my wet fur *shh it's okay heckit
I'm here*

she takes me down a long thin space and into a
bright room and she lays a soft cloth on the ground
and wraps me up in it and rolls me onto my back
and everything is a blur like my head's still
underwater

all I can see is little slaughter's big shirt

on the shirt is a yellow animal with a long neck and
I reach out and touch the animal

little slaughter says *oh this is dumb a friend gave it to
me for my birthday*

she holds my paw and moves it slowly across the
writing below the long necked animal and she says *it
says* and then she speaks to me slow in the voice
people use when they're reading out loud

not all giraffes are real

the rain is stopping says little slaughter

I'm very dry now and I try to stand and I succeed

little slaughter says *sorry you had to be down in the
cellar I don't even know what it is it's just cuz the
house is built into the hill but you're here now this is
our space*

my eyes are back to normal and I look around the
room at the soft ground and the splashes of color on
the walls and the green outside the big slabs of glass

little slaughter says *dad never comes in here*

there's another big cat across the room

oh says little slaughter and she walks over to the cat
and I follow her and the cat gets closer

we reach a hard wall and I see there are two of her
and I push my face against the hard flat cat

it's just your reflection says little slaughter

there is so much more of me here than the nose and
mouth I see in the black screens of dropped phones

I can't touch myself

little slaughter brings in a box of weird sand and
puts it in the corner and says *you can go to the
bathroom here*

I don't know what she means but I take a chance and
piss and shit in the sand and bury it and that's what
she wants and she takes the box out of the room and
brings it back fresh

this used to be for my cat says little slaughter *but he
died two years ago and dad won't let me get another
because beth is allergic to like every animal*

little slaughter shows me her sofa and tells me it's
my sofa now and I hop onto it and it's exactly my
size

she talks and I listen

I learn about longing

I get most of my new words from her

she makes a circle of sparkling stones around my
sofa and kneels and feeds me from her outstretched
palm and calls me her goddess

if you feel alone in the world

find someone to worship you

little slaughter sleeps at night and I sleep in
the day so we watch over each other

she spends most of her awake time on her phone

laughing to herself and pushing the surface with her
fingers

she holds the screen to my face and says *look heckit I
found a picture of you you're famous*

I look and it's just a bright blur

the phone shudders in her hand

ugh says little slaughter *this guy keeps texting me
he thinks just cuz we've run into each other three
times since graduation we're meant to be or
whatever but I don't believe in coincidences he can
bite my ass*

she throws the phone and I go to get it for her and
she laughs and says *leave it*

I look again at the picture

that can't be me it doesn't have a smell

I don't trust screens to tell me who I am

I'm sorry heckit says little slaughter as she
feeds me an apple because I've eaten enough
apples

*dad hasn't gone shopping cuz he's always at the
hospital I'm running out of meat for you*

even here we're in scare city

they're bringing the baby home tomorrow says little
slaughter and the way she says baby makes me
wonder if she wants to offer the baby to me for my
next meal

she says *whatever I'll be gone soon and dad'll be
happy and beth will be thrilled they can just be happy
here with their baby*

I roll sideways on the sofa and she sits with me and
rubs my head like park people rub the heads of their
dogs

am I a pet

she says *next month I'm going to santa fey to do my
photography there are a lot of witches in the desert
and I can't wait to get as far away as possible and
then I'm gonna go work at the border and take
pictures of what's really happening but I need to get
better with my spanish*

she tells me words in spanish

denada

gato

agua

in my head it's all people language

little slaughter says *you can come with me you can
eat ice*

when she's asleep I see a small set of eyes in the
darkness outside

a cat

I can't smell it but I can see blood on its little mouth
from a fresh kill

the cat looks through the glass and it looks
through me

like why aren't I out hunting why am I
inside

why isn't this person my prey

my mouth falls open and I can hear the blood inside
little slaughter

she wakes up and stands up and the cat eyes
disappear

she asks if I'm comfy

that small word

yes

and no

I lick my paws and little slaughter reads to me off
her phone

facts about big cats

she says *because of people you're becoming more and
more isolated from one another*

she says *sorry*

she reads *chronic stress can result in low reproductive
rates when in captivity*

she strokes my back and tells me about my
characteristic neck bite

I feel more like a person than ever because I'm
starting to hate myself

I look around at all the space I have and I think of
all the other space in this house and in every house
on this street and in all of ellay and I think how the
people of my town could be here too

instead of burning in the woods

this is my second room

it's so much nicer than my first

I don't belong here either

the baby comes home and cries most of the
day and night through our wall

the shouts of slaughter come home too and also
the small voice of a woman and when the woman's
small voice happens the shouts of slaughter get
softer but only for a short time

we treasure the pauses

in a long pause little slaughter sneaks chicken in to
me and I gnaw on a leg and she spends the night
telling me about a place called diznee

she tells me she wants to take me

you'd love diznee says little slaughter *there're animals
everywhere and all we have to do is jump in a car and
get on the freeway and gun it to seventy and we're
there*

I close my eyes and pictures appear

I used to want to work at diznee says little slaughter
if I worked there I'd be the evil queen but when she's
an old witch and I'd go around and scare kids
and shit

I fall asleep and have my first dream since before the
fire

when I wake up my body is moving faster
than it's ever moved

gunning it to seventy

my eyes open and the blurry distance stands still but
the world right outside the car shoots by at
unbelievable speed

my paws are up on the dashboard and I'm sitting in
the passenger seat

I turn my head and little slaughter smiles and rubs
my back as she drives

I'm so much bigger than her and my body takes up
the whole right front of the car

get excited heckit she says *we're on our way to diznee*

she lets go of me and grips the wheel

this is the long death from the inside

I look out and think I see the body of the kill sharer
but no it's a bag

other cars pass and people turn their heads and
smile and children press their little hands and faces
to the glass and scream silently

it's your birthday little slaughter says *you're turning
five and that's like thirty five in cat years*

this is your prime

it's weirdly quiet in the car like we're in a bubble
protected from the speeding world outside

the world outside slows down and our car goes up in
the air and leaves the long death below

here we are says little slaughter

we stop next to a bunch of other cars and she
jumps out and runs around and pops open my
door and my big body falls out and I'm on all four
feet again watching kids and adults and more
people than I've ever seen swarm out of their

cars and make a river of feet moving toward the
sunlight

little slaughter claps and I look up and she's
wearing a sparkling blue jumpsuit and ears like a
mouse

did she change or

we join the river of feet and we go down moving
stairs and a polished sidewalk me running
beside her

I smell something so different that it's hard to
describe and as we come to a stop and as the river of
people forms a long slow moving line I realize it's
not what I smell it's what I don't smell

no one is afraid

we reach a turnstile and I start to walk under it but a
woman says *wait*

little slaughter smiles at the woman and the woman
smiles back

is this a service animal asks the woman

yes she's my emotional support cat says little slaughter *and I have her papers right here*

she reaches in the pocket of her jumpsuit but the woman says *no you're fine*

the woman lifts my paw and presses a small wooden object gently against it

this is your hand stamp for reentry in case you leave the park says the woman

oh we won't says little slaughter *but thanks* and she moves my paw and gets her own hand stamped

now a quick picture says the woman and little slaughter turns her face and I hear an electric click from the device

now her turn says the woman and little slaughter grasps my neck and tilts my face up and says *smile for the picture heckit* and I do I smile

the only time a cat has done that

music and voices are everywhere inside the gates

there are other animals big animals with soft fur
and faces and they stand upright and hug and blend
in with the people all the people the people with
their own ears and hats and bright objects and no
one thinks I'm strange at all

and some of the kids come over and pet me and
little slaughter lets them and they say *she's beautiful*
and little slaughter says *it's her birthday* and the kids
tie a birthday ribbon around my neck and we walk
down the wide main street together

there's a bench beneath a castle and little slaughter
sits me down there and says *stay*

I stay and enjoy my stillness within all the motion
around me

as soon as I get hungry food appears

a huge bird leg that little slaughter holds out to
me and she has her own and she sits down on the
bench and she tears into the fat flesh

I look around and others are eating these big ugly
meats too so I slobber and chew and join in

gory gory feasting

so far from scare city

you must be this tall to ride says little slaughter in the reading voice

she stands by a sideways stick in the air and holds her hand out to measure its height

stand up heckit she says and I stand up like the other big animals in diznee and now my neck is above the sideways stick

I'm a good emotional support cat and I'll be tall for her

perfect says little slaughter and we run to the front of the line and they strap us into a log and water sloshes over the sides and she clutches my back and the ride begins

there's darkness and color and animals singing and animals being tortured and each time we go over a cliff my stomach slams up into my throat and I feel amazing

when we get off the ride we're soaked so I shake
myself dry and everyone around us screams and
enjoys the water raining off me

look heckit there we are says little slaughter and she
points to a screen and I see the screen clearly and on
it we're going down the big cliff and little slaughter
has her hands up and her hands block the faces of
the people in the ride behind us and I look so scared
of my own happiness

I love the photos says little slaughter *now even if we
leave we'll still be here*

we wait in a line surrounded by glowing wooden
statues

it reminds me of the forest when I was a kitten when
I loved the sunlight and there was more green than
there ever would be again

this is worth it says little slaughter *it's my favorite
thing in the world*

the glowing wooden statues shake and make
noise

that one's the goddess of fire says little slaughter as we step forward

and this one causes earthquakes

she touches a branch and it sings

these trees are alive and fake

the line moves again and little slaughter gets her favorite thing in the world

it's yellow and cold and she holds one for both of us and licks hers and says *mmmm* and holds mine out for me but she holds it up high and says *okay heckit if you want this you have to stand up again and stay standing* and I do what she says again and like magic I'm fully upright licking too

I'm taller than little slaughter now

we walk through more forests fake and real and out into a fantasy

and the day fades to night and the lights come on at the castle and more transformation happens

I look at her and she looks at me and she's no longer
in a jumpsuit and mouse ears no she's changed
again when I wasn't looking and she's wearing a
dark dress and a jeweled crown

I'm on two legs and it feels permanent

a person in a cat suit

my paws drop to my sides and they're ready to grasp

little slaughter says *I'm the queen now the evil queen
and you're my emotional support goddess*

we pass a line of people shuffling like there's
something great at the end and as we get to the end I
see a throne and a sofa at the top of some stairs and
I know the throne is for little slaughter and the sofa
is for me

up there is where we belong

at the top of the stairs we take our places

little slaughter seated and clutching the arms of the
throne like she was born there and me sprawled out

the whole length of the sofa scratching its fabric and
licking my paws to a regal polish

the people at the front of the line come to us and
pose

a photographer flashes picture after picture and
everyone who comes up and stands with us smiles
because they know that the photos mean even after
they leave they'll still be here

the line moves but stays just as large and it stretches
into the distance and for once I can see the
distance instead of the usual blur and I can see all
the way over the diznee buildings and across the
faraway lights of ellay and I can see the dark
mountains below the hollywood sign where I think
I must be must be asleep and dreaming this

because how

more flashes come from the camera and more
smiles come from the people assembled
around us

the birthday ribbon around my neck swells and I
want to speak

so I do

at the sound of my voice the stairs shift and start to
move forward

the throne and sofa are now the top of a parade float

costumed animals appear and begin the parade and
our float follows

our people below part to both sides of the wide
street and they cheer and take their own pictures
and wave their huge bird legs and twirl their shining
sticks

pinks and reds like sparks of blood and thought

our people shower us with cheers as we reach the
end of the main street and I see the exit and think
no no don't let it be over

the float slowly turns around so we can face back the
way we came

look up says little slaughter *look all the way up*

I tilt my spinning head back

fireworks

the fireworks explode in the shape of little
slaughter's face and explode in the shape of my face
and in the night sky we're smiling exactly like we
smiled in the photos they took at the turnstiles

I look at little slaughter's real face lit up by her
firework face and she rubs my head

a storm of eyes is on us from our people below

I lift my goddess paw and wave at them and they all
wave back

we're here heckit we made it says little slaughter *we're
in the happiest place on earth*

our sky faces fall apart and rain down and leave
smoke

the scream that fills my ears lets me know that I'm waking up for real

diznee is gone and I'm back in little slaughter's room

a woman stands in the doorway and she's making the scream

she gasps and then she is quieter than I thought a person could be

she holds a big sucking machine on the floor and it makes a big sucking sound

until she slides it at me fast and hard and it knocks the table next to my sofa and stops making a sucking sound and the lamp falls off onto the carpet and breaks into pieces

I look at the woman and she is frozen like she's expecting me to move first to indulge her I lick a paw

clean and peaceful

she runs away and I hear more of her screams and I
feel powerful and also guilty as fuck

I look at the lamp in pieces on the floor

I can't fix this

I have no idea what it's like to be a person and to be
confronted with a me

the carpet is ruined already by the shards of lamp so
I get down off my sofa and scratch and scratch at it
and try to claw words into the floor to explain
myself

but when I climb back onto the sofa and look down
at my work it's jagged strips with no order or
meaning

someday I'll be able to write what you're reading

maybe in santa fey with little slaughter

telling every word to her

or on the other side of the world from the burning
hills

in new york with a therapist

maybe I'll write it from an okay future a future
where I'm safe

or maybe it won't ever get written

only growled

little slaughter enters the room and the room feels
right again with her in it

but she is acting wrong

shit shit she says *I'm so sorry heckit I forgot that
marie comes mondays fuck*

she sits on the sofa and I jump up and lay out
and put my head in her lap and she pets me for
a sec before standing and leaving me for her
drawers

*okay okay we're just gonna have to go to santa fey
early* she says

I can see the decision in her eyes and in the way she
grabs a bag and unzips it and tears open every
drawer and stuffs clothes and shoes into the bag

*what do you need heckit you need food lots of food
okay okay* little slaughter says and each word gets
faster as it comes out

she comes back over to me and puts her forehead to
my forehead

you didn't do anything bad she says *you're perfect I
just fucked up*

there's the sound of a car outside and little slaughter
freezes like marie froze when she saw me

her tiny fear voice says *dad's home*

this is slaughter the man not just slaughter the
voice

but his voice came in with him and it fills the room

jane get back he says to little slaughter and grabs her
and pulls her toward the door and she throws him
off and comes back to me and he yells *goddammit do
what I say*

slaughter is smaller than I expected and he has only
a little bit of hair on his head and the little bit of hair
he has is white

he's holding a long smooth stick in one fist and he
points it at me

get away from it he yells *jane come over here*

little slaughter puts her hands on her hips and
doesn't move

he slams the door and locks it behind him and says
*beth is calling the cops jane this is serious you need to
come over here with me*

the air in the room is hot with slaughter here

it's a cougar jane he says *it's a goddamn cougar*

is that what I am

the door jiggles and bangs

slaughter flattens his body against it and he checks
that it's locked

a woman's voice comes from behind the door
shouting *what's going on jack I just saw marie
take off*

did you call the cops slaughter yells at the door and
the door yells *call them and tell them what*

just go be with the baby yells slaughter and then he
turns to little slaughter and says *jesus jane the baby
the baby's here*

little slaughter stays still and I stay still with her and
we could be a picture we're so not moving

slaughter looks around the room and sees the
broken lamp and the mess of drawers and he says
the first quiet thing I've heard him say he says *why is
your suitcase out*

you wanna have a baby dad fine yells little
slaughter *you wanna date a baby fine but I get a
fucking baby too*

I'm not the problem now yells slaughter *you are the
problem now this is the problem*

he points the stick at me and I notice his throat

look shouts little slaughter *she's mine she's okay*

slaughter holds the stick with both hands and steps
forward

little slaughter holds her hands out flat in front of
her like it will add to her power

she's not gonna bite me says little slaughter

she puts her head by my mouth and I don't
bite her

she's not gonna claw me

she lifts my paw up to her side and I don't claw her
and she lets go and I drop my paw and dangle it off
the sofa in the least scary way I can

she won't even move

I don't even move

slaughter's hands turn purple he's gripping the stick hard

I try to purr and it comes out wrong

I'm so good but things don't get better

how long have you had this in the house jane

forever dad for fucking ever

jane get over here

what

jane this isn't okay

dad put the bat away you don't need it she's good

you keep saying she she what the hell jane

yeah dad this is heckit she's mine and I'm hers

I can see its goddamn dick

fuck you

jane

fuck that and fuck you dad

little slaughter rushes forward and unlocks the door
and slaughter runs to stop her and lets the stick fall
to his side and little slaughter is gone and another
person replaces her in the doorway and says *jack
what the fuck is going on with your daughter*

beth wait says slaughter

the new woman sees me and of course the new
woman freezes everyone freezes or runs those are
the two things everyone does except for little
slaughter and I want her in here but she's not here
where did she go

jack it's the mountain lion says the new woman *what*
says slaughter *it's theee mountain lion you haven't
read about it it lives in the park*

is this fame

well now it's fucking here says slaughter and the
woman says *jack we have a baby* and then the

woman does the other thing that everyone does she
runs

slaughter raises the stick again but he steps
backward instead of forward and reaches out a hand
to grip the doorknob and starts to slowly close the
door

a scream happens

jack shouts the woman from down the hall *jack
where's the baby the baby's gone*

slaughter runs after her down the hall and takes his
shouting with him

I have a moment to think

after searching my head I don't have any thoughts
and I use my eyes and I look over at the reflection on
the closet doors

in the room inside the glass I see an unplugged
sucking machine on its side

I see a shattered lamp on the floor

I see rips in the carpet from claws

I see an open suitcase and drawers pulled out

I see the green blur of trees behind the sofa

I see a circle of stones and cards and candles

I see myself

I see myself

it's time to leave

little slaughter runs back in with a full backpack and
slams the door and locks it

she runs to me and holds me tight

don't worry heckit she says *the baby's fine I just
moved his little bed thing into the laundry room
so we've got like fifteen minutes till they find him
but he's good he's got his little binky and
everything*

I don't worry about the baby

little slaughter stuffs one more pile of clothes into
her suitcase and throws the backpack over her
shoulder

she jingles keys at me like it's a game

it's not a game

here we go she says and she runs to the glass wall
behind the sofa and pushes it to the side and pats
her leg and I go over to her

she gestures for me to move forward and I do

there's nothing between me and the outside

I'm stretched across the back seat and little
slaughter is driving

I have some room back here

stay down says little slaughter *stay down for now
okay*

I feel the car speeding and turning and
turning

then we stop and I almost roll off the seat and I claw
my way back up to sitting

shit says little slaughter and the car moves very
slowly stopping and starting and it's not at all like
the speed of my diznee dream

the car is a quiet bubble though and I enjoy the quiet
after the screaming and running and breaking in
the slaughter house

traffic it's traffic heckit she says *it's going to take us a while to get out of this and hit the freeway*

little slaughter drums her fingers on the steering wheel and the car edges forward

I can see her reflection and her eyes are angry and afraid but smiling at me

she says *now we're stuck here getting cancer like everybody else*

when we come to a full stop again little slaughter takes her hands off the wheel and grabs a bag and rips it open and turns around in her seat and pours chunks of dried meat out in front of me

I eat them

good girl says little slaughter

it's nice to be fed and praised at the same time

I wish you could talk back to me says little slaughter and she faces forward and the car moves again and she keeps talking *fucking rush owwer of course clear keep it says on the street clear and then keep in that order when you're going slow that's how I always read it*

I nod but I don't know what she's talking about and she meets my eyes again in the reflection and she watches me swallow and reaches back and touches my leg

say something she says *please heckit I'm not talking to myself for this entire drive so just say something*

I want to

I open my mouth

okay fuck this says little slaughter *we're going through the neighborhood*

she turns the wheel and we speed right and for a moment we're going faster but then we stop again and little slaughter bangs a hand on the steering wheel and sinks her head against it

she turns and caresses my back and I can feel her frustration in every pet

*really stay down now heckit there's people everywhere
here I'm sorry but you have to stay down and don't
look out*

I love her and I'm thankful for the time we've spent
together

whether she summoned me or I found her

I'm excited for her image of our future

a life far away

I let her pet me harder than I want to be petted

and I listen close when she says *stay down stay down*

but when she lets go and looks away I do the opposite

from inside the car I see all the people

some walk and some sit and they all hold phones
and tap on them

and at the tables that take up most of the sidewalk
across the street the people drink and eat and
talk and don't talk

there is a lot going on but all I see is one person
alone at a table in the middle of all the tables and it's
a person I know

it's a neck I know

the man with the whip

I watch his neck that familiar neck but I also watch
his hands they move up and down as he eats and I
think of how easily those hands can make fire and
how easily that fire can destroy tents and a town and
burn a forest

every person sitting and walking has hands too and
I see all their hands and I know what their hands
can do and what their hands would do and the
violence waiting behind every motion

I learn something new

I learn I can open a car door

on quiet midnights back in the caves I could
almost imagine that all the people were gone

canyons cleared of their footsteps and voices and
cars

the long deaths standing still

trees expanding and their green swallowing the
buildings and returning the original smells

returning what's needed

I could see myself leaving the park and walking
through an empty ellay

slow and safe with all the other animals

back to the deep forest and the forever water and the
sun setting

people can't see it but I can

their end makes everything okay

scare city isn't scare city with no one around to say
its name

I open the car door and jump out onto the
street and it's only a street only a short
death and I cross it quickly with the cars
all stopped

when I reach the man with the whip there are fewer
people because they've dropped their bags and
kicked their chairs and run away

but the man with the whip doesn't see me until I'm
in leaping distance

and so I leap and my claws connect with his chest
and I knock him back and he falls out of his
chair and his face hits the sidewalk and his nose
sprays blood

he rolls over and looks up and I'm pinning him
down

where's your whip now I think where's your fire

his neck vein bulges like a wish come true

I can smell his blood on the pavement and I'm not at all hungry

this is not about need

no this is want

it's a terrible choice but I'm making it

just like a person

my teeth tear into his neck tear right through the vein and my jaws clamp and twist and do what they're meant to do and his body cracks under my weight and he stops moving

his blood fills my stomach

warm rain

I look up and my head clears and I remember little slaughter

she's the only person outside and she's standing in the middle of the street by her open car doors her eyes are on my eyes and

my eyes shoot fireworks

she sees the dead man and she sees that I made him
that way and her fists clench and she shudders like
an earthquake

we meet for the first time

hello little slaughter

this is what a goddess looks like

she steps back and slams the door that I opened and
she gives me one last glance

I would only slow you down little slaughter

you've got so many miles to go

she gets in the front seat and shuts the door

good girl

I look down at the man with the whip who is now
the man with no whip and no life

I look down at his open throat

his hands aren't hands anymore they're just useless
hunks of white

little slaughter starts the car

I'm letting her go

there's blood all over my body

my mother would be so proud

little slaughter's car finds an opening and she speeds
away

a big car sound replaces her little car sound in
the air

many cars and their mechanical howls coming
closer and

then I hear the sky sound I remember from the
mountain a fucking helicopter

not a rescue chopper to carry me somewhere safe

but the kind that circles close and blinds with its
light

I hear the whirring and it gets louder than the cars
and I know the sound is coming for me and the
people inside the sound are coming for me

there's nowhere to go

I'm done with thickets and caves and rooms and I'm
sick of being outside

I step away from my prey

his thick empty body is too heavy to hide

I'm only sorry I didn't get to eat all of you

the howling cars form a mess in the street

lights swirl everywhere

padded people leave the cars and surround me and
point long objects

these aren't sticks

they shout so loud at one another that I can't tell
what they're saying

I can't listen anymore

the fucking helicopter's whirring is right above us
and the padded people look up and then look back
at me and what I see in their eyes is what they see in
mine

a threat

I retract my claws and try to become the kitten at
the center of my self

maybe the padded people know why I did what I did

maybe they understand

I say something

it sounds like words

it's not what they want to hear

ACKNOWLEDGMENTS

Ferocious gratitude:

To Kate Durbin, without whom I wouldn't know Los Angeles in all of its kaleidoscopic chaos, and Emma Rathbone, who helped this book find its champions.

To Jim Rutman, Szilvia Molnar, Brooke Ehrlich, and the amazing team at Sterling Lord Literistic, for making a lifelong dream come true.

To Lee, who called heckit by name, and Millicent, who didn't eat the rat.

To Johanna Hedva ("do not fuck with my syntax") and Katherine Faw ("just the best ones"), for guiding me through a whirlwind.

To Jackson Howard and Gillian Fitzgerald-Kelly, who brought this animal out of the wilderness, and everyone at MCD / Farrar, Straus and Giroux and Picador. I worship you.

To the wondrous friends, collaborators, and colleagues who supported me all these weird years of leaving, staying put, and returning as a fictional beast. We know who we are.

To my family, for y'all's constant care in uncaring times.

To Malcolm, for all my stored-up souls.

To Merkel, magical navigatrix on our life's journey through art. Love beyond all words. You're my favorite writer, and my favorite human.

This book is for P-22, who walks beside me in dreams, and Jane, who turned the pages.

A NOTE ABOUT THE AUTHOR

Henry Hoke is an editor at *The Offing* and a writer whose work has appeared in *No Tokens*, *Triangle House Review*, *Electric Literature*, and the flash noir anthology *Tiny Crimes*. He co-created the performance series Enter>text in Los Angeles and has taught at CalArts and the UVA Young Writers Workshop. He lives in New York City.